To Carolin and the gang – **M.B.**

ORCHARD BOOKS

First published in Great Britain in 2020
by The Watts Publishing Group

10 9 8 7 6 5 4 3 2 1

Text and illustrations © Magda Brol, 2020

The moral rights of the author-illustrator
have been asserted.

All rights reserved.

A CIP catalogue record for this book is
available from the British Library.

HB ISBN 978 1 40835 089 8
PB ISBN 978 1 40835 091 1

Printed and bound in China

Orchard Books
An imprint of Hachette Children's Group
Part of The Watts Publishing Group Limited
Carmelite House, 50 Victoria Embankment
London EC4Y 0DZ

An Hachette UK Company
www.hachette.co.uk

www.hachettechildrens.co.uk

MIX
Paper from
responsible sources
FSC
www.fsc.org
FSC® C104740

Once upon a Penguin

Magda Brol

ORCHARD

One day, on a cold and remote iceberg, Paco the Penguin stumbled upon . . .

. . . SOMETHING.

It was **big** and **red** and **flippy-flappy** in the middle.

Was it a **roof?**

A **raft?**

A **glider?**

A windbreaker?

A bottom warmer?

A hat?

The **Thing** didn't do very much and the other penguins quickly lost interest.

But Paco's
curiosity grew
and grew.

He stared at the
big red flippy-
flappy thing,
trying hard to
figure it out …

cat

c

apple

t

s

e

and as
the days, then
weeks, went by,
the little marks
started to
make sense.

B   3

(Paco was a VERY clever penguin.)

From that day on, Paco always had his head buried deep in the Thing.

When the other penguins looked for shelter, he'd say, "I'm on a tropical island. There's no snow here."

At dinnertime, he'd say, "I'm not hungry! I'm eating ice cream with a princess!"

And at bedtime, he'd say, "I can't go to bed yet! We are flying to the moon in a spaceship."

The penguins were very confused.
A tropical island? A princess? A spaceship …

WHERE?

"It's all in here," explained Paco. "Inside the big red flippy-flappy thing. **Listen!**"

So Paco began to tell them about . . .

amazing people,

faraway lands,

and magical creatures.

It was exciting,

surprising,

and sometimes a little scary!

And when he turned the very last page . . .

"We want more!"

cried the penguins.

"There isn't any more," said Paco sadly.

"There is only one big red flippy-flappy thing."

But wait a minute, what was this?

"Property of Anton Library," read Paco.

"Who's Anton Library?" asked the penguins.

"I don't know, but let's find him! He might have more big red flippy-flappy things!"

The penguins liked the idea
very much. So off they went . . .

across the sea . . .

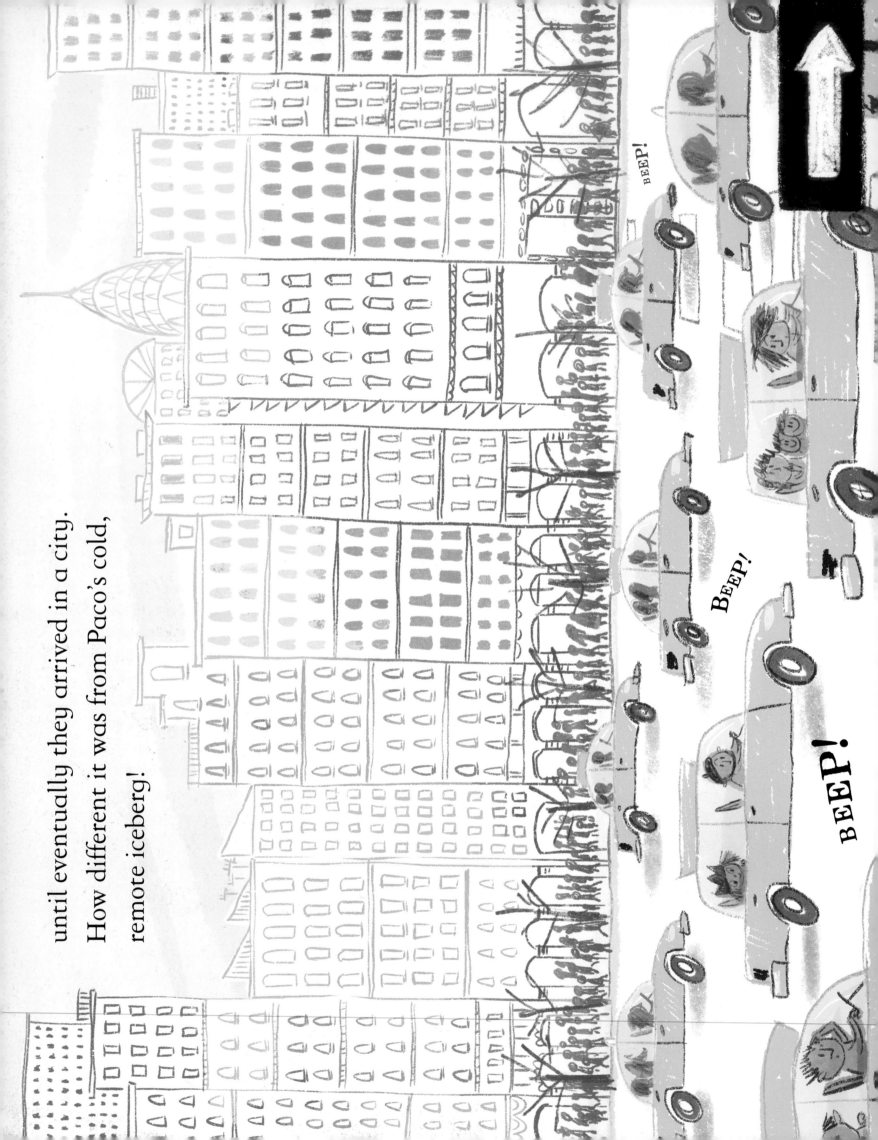

until eventually they arrived in a city. How different it was from Paco's cold, remote iceberg!

BEEP!

BEEP!

BEEP!

BEEP!

It was crowded and noisy
and everyone waddled so fast!

"Why won't anyone STOP?!" cried Paco.

But suddenly they spotted a familiar face...

"PRINCESS!"

who took them to Anton Library.

Anton Library was NOT what the penguins
had expected. No legs! No arms! No head!
Anton Library wasn't a person at all.

But it did have lots of big
flippy-flappy things – in
all different colours.

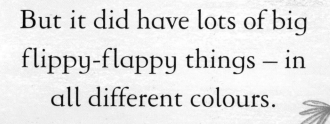

"These are BOOKS!"

said the princess.

"Let's read!"

So they did.

Right until closing time . . .

Once upon a penguin . . .

"Closing time?" cried Paco.
"But **I HAVE** to know how this story ends!"

"You can take it home," said the princess. "**Everyone** can borrow books from a library!"

And as more
and more books
travelled back and
forth, Paco's little
rock no longer
seemed cold
and remote.

All thanks . . .

...to a **big red flippy-flappy thing**.